The GUMBY™ Book of Numbers

Jane Hyman

DOUBLEDAY & COMPANY, INC.
GARDEN CITY, NEW YORK

D1508694

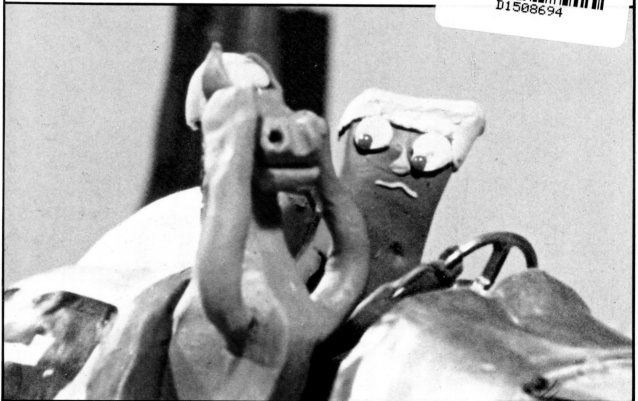

For the Donovan School PTO, which has supported me in so many educational endeavors

Library of Congress Cataloging-in-Publication Data

Hyman, Jane.
    The Gumby book of numbers.

    Summary: Clay figures Gumby and Pokey introduce the concepts of counting and matching objects to corresponding numerals.
    1. Number concept—Juvenile literature.   [1. Number concept.   2. Counting]   I. Title.
QA141.15.H96   1986   513'.2 [E]   86–6193
ISBN 0-385-23455-4 Trade
ISBN 0-385-23847-9 Lib. bdg.

For Grown-Ups

Do you remember Gumby? He's that little green blob of clay who brings fun and enjoyment to children of all ages. Let Gumby help you spend some quality time with your child as you both discover that learning with Gumby and his friends can be creative and rewarding.

Pick a special place that's comfortable and peaceful. Keep all distractions to a minimum. Perhaps you'll want to set aside a specific time each day for you and your youngster to read the book together. Make this a private time between you and your child. You both deserve to learn from each other.

This number book has been designed to expose your child to the concept of matching objects to the corresponding numerals. For example, there will be a photograph of five men sitting around a table with the numeral "5" written on the same page. You might want to reinforce this one-to-one correspondence by counting some concrete objects in your home. You can use buttons, spoons, or almost any safe object to count.

Have a wonderful time together. Remember, you are your child's first teacher and your home is your youngster's first school. Enjoy!

Gumby and his friend Pokey
were ready to play the racing
game.

They jumped in their car and
got set to go.

The man called out the rules
of the game.

When the gun was fired, the race began!

1 Poor Gumby and Pokey! Their **one** and only engine was choking. They had to start over again.

There were **two** blockheads in the race with Gumby and Pokey.

2

3 Look. There are **three** cars
in the lead.

Do you think Gumby and Pokey
will win? Pokey is too busy
looking at things along the side
of the road. He'd better watch
the race.

4 "Look at the **four** pieces of clothes on the clothesline," Pokey said.

"And there are **five** men sitting around a table. I wonder what they're saying."

5

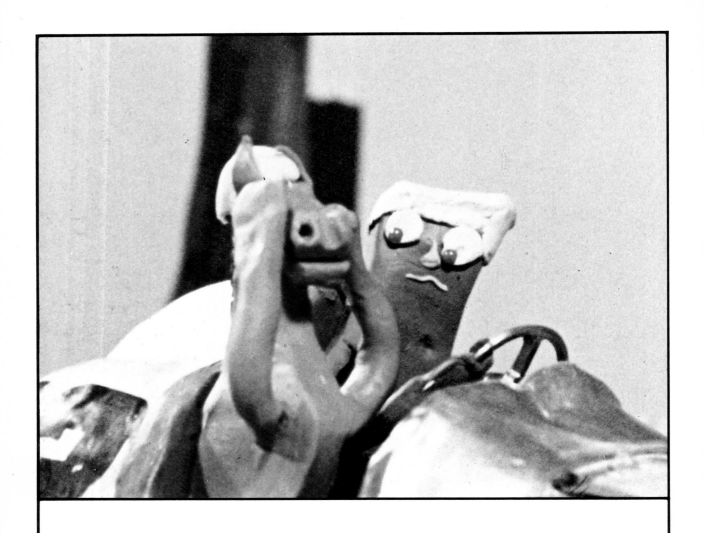

"Pokey, keep your eyes on the road. I need your help," Gumby said.

The **six** blockheads in the
pit stop are trying to help
the blockheads win the race.

6

"Pokey, *please* keep your eyes
on the road," Gumby cried.

"But look at that accordion.
It has **seven** black keys,"
Pokey replied.

7

"And that xylophone has **eight** different keys. What great music we could make!"

8

9

"Look over there. I think I
see nine baby gophers,"
Pokey said.

"Here comes their father.
Now there are **ten** gophers
in all."

10

"Pokey, please pay attention
to the race. We might lose,"
Gumby said.

Gumby and Pokey crossed
the finish line first!

They won first prize in the race.

And that's the end of the
racing game.

TIME CLOCK

Look at the time clock that was used in the race. Point to the number **one**. Can you find the number **five**? What is the new number on this clock? What other numbers do you see?